JUSTICE LEAGUE

VERSUS

DC COMICS™

WRITTEN BY
JOHN SAZAKLIS
AND
STEVE FOXE

SCHOLASTIC

Produced by becker&mayer!
11120 NE 33rd Place, Suite 101
Bellevue, WA 98004
www.beckermayer.com

becker&mayer!
BOOK PRODUCERS

If you have questions or comments about this product, please visit
www.beckermayer/customerservice and click on Customer Service Request Form.

Edited by Delia Greve
Designed by Sam Dawson
Production management by Cindy Curran

Printed, manufactured, and assembled in Shenzhen, China
First printing, January 2016

10 9 8 7 6 5 4 3 2 1   16 17 18 19 20

ISBN 978-0-545-89062-5

15072

Design textures used throughout: Paper texture © ilolab/Shutterstock; metal texture © Waj/
Shutterstock; metal texture © caesart/Shutterstock; metal background © Igorsky/Shutterstock.
Page 21: Rainforest © Tithi Luadthong. Page 29: Forest © Tithi Luadthong. Page 31: Entrance
gate © Unholy Vault Designs.

TABLE OF CONTENTS

4

WHAT IS THE JUSTICE LEAGUE 6

GREEN LANTERN (JOHN STEWART) vs THE JOKER 8

WONDER WOMAN vs ATROCITUS 10

NIGHTWING vs CATWOMAN 12

GREEN LANTERN (HAL JORDAN) vs CAPTAIN COLD

CYBORG vs MAN-BAT 14

FIRESTORM vs FIREFLY 16

ZATANNA vs SCARECROW 18

RED ARROW vs POISON IVY 20

THE FLASH vs BANE 22

ROBIN vs HUSH 24

SUPER-VILLAINS SUPREME 26

HAWKGIRL vs CHEETAH 28

BLACK LIGHTNING vs KILLER CROC 30

BATWOMAN vs RĀ'S AL GHŪL 32

SUPERMAN vs ARES 34

BLACK CANARY vs HARLEY QUINN 36

RED TORNADO vs DEADSHOT 38

HUNTRESS vs TWO-FACE 40

MARTIAN MANHUNTER vs BIZARRO 42

VIXEN vs THE PENGUIN 44

BATMAN vs LEX LUTHOR 46

EXPERT PICKS 48

WHAT IS THE

SUPERMAN is vulnerable to Kryptonite, a radioactive element from his home planet Krypton. Green Kryptonite makes him weak, while red can cause mutations.

THE FLASH's control of the Speed Force allows him to travel through time and even into other dimensions!

WONDER WOMAN's Golden Lasso of Truth was forged by the smith god Hephaestus. Any living creature caught by it is compelled to tell the truth.

SUPERMAN

BLACK CANARY

GREEN LANTERN (John Stewart)

THE FLASH

WONDER WOMAN

WHEN EARTH was threatened by a menace from beyond the stars, Superman, Batman, Wonder Woman, Green Lantern, The Flash, and other brave heroes answered the call, banding together to repel the alien threat and save humanity. These courageous beings have vowed to stand together as the Justice League to serve and protect mankind!

Before joining the Justice League, **BLACK LIGHTNING** worked alongside the Outsiders, a group of misfit heroes formed by Batman.

BATMAN traveled the globe and trained for years under the world's greatest martial artists, detectives, and spies. He donned the guise of a bat to strike fear into the hearts of criminals.

GREEN LANTERN
(Hal Jordan)

MARTIAN MANHUNTER

BLACK LIGHTNING

HAWKGIRL

BATMAN

GREEN LANTERN (JOHN STEWART) VS THE JOKER

GREEN LANTERN
(JOHN STEWART)

Former U.S. Marine John Stewart took up the role of Earth's Green Lantern when Hal Jordan, the previous ring-bearer, was injured in battle. His training as an architect gives him an edge when it comes to constructing objects with the ring's hard-light energy.

SECRET FILE

Real Name	John Stewart
Weapons	Green Lantern power ring
Occupation	Former U.S. Marine, architect
Height	6'1"
Weight	200 lbs
Special Powers	Ability to create hard-light energy constructs

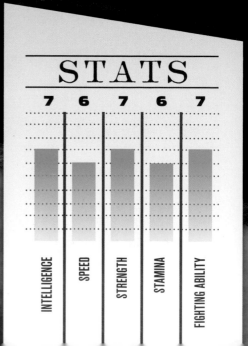

STATS

INTELLIGENCE	SPEED	STRENGTH	STAMINA	FIGHTING ABILITY
7	6	7	6	7

SHOWDOWN

John Stewart arrives to find the asylum staff laughing uncontrollably due to the effects of Joker Venom. The Joker promptly locks down the facility—shutting John Stewart inside as well! The Joker's voice echoes over the intercom, threatening to free the inmates. John Stewart lights his power ring and flies off to find the criminal clown.

THE JOKER

The Joker's true origins are a mystery, but one thing is certain: this crooked clown's crimes are no laughing matter.

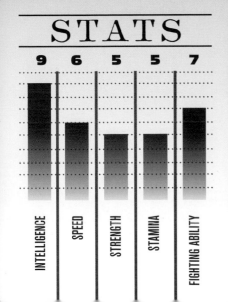

STATS

INTELLIGENCE	SPEED	STRENGTH	STAMINA	FIGHTING ABILITY
9	6	5	5	7

SECRET FILE

Real Name	Unknown
Weapons	Joker Venom, acid-spitting flowers
Occupation	Chaotic criminal mastermind
Height	6'5"
Weight	192 lbs
Special Powers	Immunity to his own toxins

WONDER WOMAN VS ATROCITUS

THE SETUP!

Wonder Woman's visit to her peaceful island home of Themyscira is interrupted when Atrocitus, the ruthless alien leader of the Red Lanterns, crash-lands on the island. Armed with her Golden Lasso of Truth, Wonder Woman must defend her home against the rampaging Red Lantern.

WONDER WOMAN

As an Amazon ambassador of peace and justice, Wonder Woman puts her warrior training to use. Wonder Woman won the right to leave Themyscira in a contest of champions and is a founding member of the Justice League.

SECRET FILE

Real Name	Diana Prince
Weapons	Golden Lasso of Truth, boomerang tiara, bulletproof wrist gauntlets
Occupation	Ambassador of peace and justice
Height	6'0"
Weight	165 lbs
Special Powers	Mythical strength, speed, agility, flight, accelerated healing

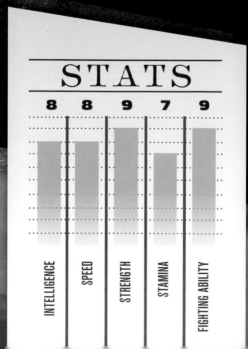

STATS

INTELLIGENCE	SPEED	STRENGTH	STAMINA	FIGHTING ABILITY
8	8	9	7	9

SHOWDOWN

Shaking with rage, Atrocitus pulls himself from the fiery wreckage of his ship only to face Wonder Woman. When Atrocitus begins lashing out at Wonder Woman's fellow Amazons, the warrior princess takes swift action. She must restrain the Red Lantern with her lasso before his anger makes him too powerful to control.

ATROCITUS

Atrocitus lost everything when the rogue Manhunter robots rampaged across his home planet of Ryut. With nothing left to lose, Atrocitus became the perfect vessel for the rage of the Red Lantern.

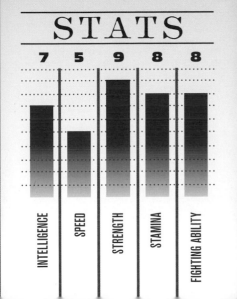

STATS

7	5	9	8	8
INTELLIGENCE	SPEED	STRENGTH	STAMINA	FIGHTING ABILITY

Real Name	Atros
Weapons	Red Lantern power ring
Occupation	Leader of the Red Lantern Corps
Height	8'0"
Weight	650 lbs
Special Powers	Super-strength, the ability to generate hard-light energy constructs

NIGHTWING VS CATWOMAN

THE SETUP!

While on patrol, Nightwing spots a hole cut into the skylight of a penthouse. The agile hero is about to investigate when a nimble figure streaks out of the hole. It's Catwoman! Hefting a sack of stolen goods on her shoulder, the cunning cat burglar flees across the rooftop.

NIGHTWING

Like his mentor, Bruce Wayne, circus performer Dick Grayson lost his parents to crime at an early age. Taken under Batman's wing, Dick adopted the mantle of Robin, Batman's sidekick, before establishing his own identity as Nightwing.

SECRET FILE

Real Name	Richard "Dick" Grayson
Weapons	Escrima sticks
Occupation	Acrobat
Height	5'10"
Weight	175 lbs
Special Powers	Expert agility, self-defense skills

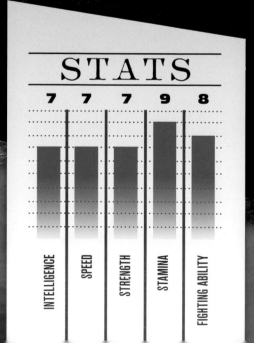

STATS

INTELLIGENCE	SPEED	STRENGTH	STAMINA	FIGHTING ABILITY
7	7	7	9	8

SHOWDOWN

Catwoman leaps from building to building, just out of the reach of Nightwing. Thinking fast, Nightwing hurls one of his escrima sticks at Catwoman's bag, sending it plummeting into a Dumpster below. Baring her claws, the feline foe turns to face her pursuer!

CATWOMAN

Selina Kyle often finds herself on the wrong side of the law but always for a good cause. Her thievery gives her an uneasy relationship with Batman, yet she is one of the few people he trusts with his secret identity.

STATS

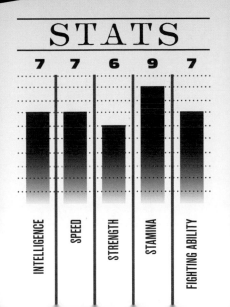

INTELLIGENCE	SPEED	STRENGTH	STAMINA	FIGHTING ABILITY
7	7	6	9	7

SECRET FILE

Real Name	Selina Kyle
Weapons	Razor-sharp claws, a bullwhip
Occupation	Thief, vigilante
Height	5'7"
Weight	133 lbs
Special Powers	Masterful acrobatics, fighting prowess

GREEN LANTERN VS CAPTAIN COLD
(HAL JORDAN)

THE SETUP! Upon returning from the planet Oa, Green Lantern Corps member Hal Jordan discovers the sub-zero Rogue Captain Cold has frozen the busy streets of Coast City, trapping hundreds of civilians in a sheet of ice.

GREEN LANTERN
(HAL JORDAN)

From the first time he put on the power ring, fearless test pilot Hal Jordan gained a new sense of purpose. As a member of the Green Lantern Corps, Hal Jordan splits his time between space and Earth.

STATS

7	6	7	6	7
INTELLIGENCE	SPEED	STRENGTH	STAMINA	FIGHTING ABILITY

SECRET FILE

Real Name	Hal Jordan
Weapons	Green Lantern power ring
Occupation	Pilot
Height	6'2"
Weight	186 lbs
Special Powers	Great willpower, ability to create hard-light energy constructs

SHOWDOWN

Knowing his frost is no match for Green Lantern's power ring, Cold creates a diversion. He aims his icy weapon at a school bus full of children and innocent bystanders. Green Lantern forms a magnifying glass to redirect the sun's rays, but Captain Cold moves to make his escape.

CAPTAIN COLD

Leader of the Rogues, enemies of The Flash, Captain Cold is a villain with a loose sense of honor. Armed with his ice-generating cold guns, Captain Cold has been known to freeze heroes in their tracks!

STATS

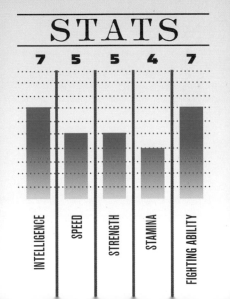

7	INTELLIGENCE
5	SPEED
5	STRENGTH
4	STAMINA
7	FIGHTING ABILITY

SECRET FILE

Real Name	Leonard Snart
Weapons	Sub-zero cold guns
Occupation	Criminal
Height	6'2"
Weight	196 lbs
Special Powers	Cold guns can shoot ice and lower the temperature to dangerous levels

CYBORG VS MAN-BAT

THE SETUP! Cyborg is watching his favorite team play at the Hub City football stadium when a harried Man-Bat crashes onto the field. Dazed and confused by the bright lights, the doctor lashes out at the players around him. Cyborg leaps onto the turf to contain Man-Bat.

CYBORG

After a devastating lab accident, Victor Stone was forced to give up his promising athletic career. His scientist father rebuilt his body with experimental robotics, giving life to Cyborg!

SECRET FILE

Real Name	Victor Stone
Weapons	Sonic disruptor, laser gauntlets
Occupation	Former college athlete
Height	6'6"
Weight	340 lbs
Special Powers	Adaptive cybernetic body, advanced weapons system

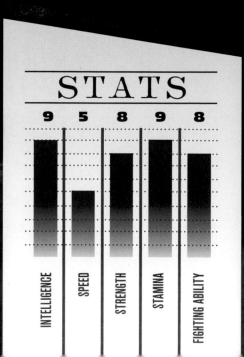

STATS

INTELLIGENCE	SPEED	STRENGTH	STAMINA	FIGHTING ABILITY
9	5	8	9	8

SHOWDOWN

Man-Bat's animal instincts make him dangerous and unpredictable—especially when he feels threatened. Cyborg fires a few stun lasers from his cybernetic arm, but the risk of hitting fans in the stands is too high. Left with only his sonic disruptor, Cyborg must subdue Man-Bat before the end zone becomes a danger zone!

MAN-BAT

In an attempt to cure his hearing loss by tapping into bats' amazing sonar abilities, Dr. Kirk Langstrom created a serum from the nocturnal animals' glands. Instead of curing him, however, the serum turned Langstrom into an uncontrollable human/bat hybrid!

STATS

	4	8	8	6	7

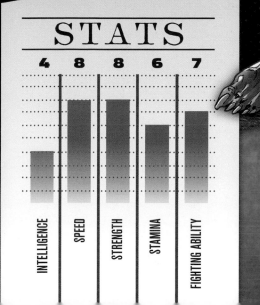

INTELLIGENCE · SPEED · STRENGTH · STAMINA · FIGHTING ABILITY

SECRET FILE

Real Name	Dr. Kirk Langstrom
Weapons	Sharp claws and teeth
Occupation	Biologist
Height	7'4"
Weight	315 lbs
Special Powers	Enhanced strength, flight, sonar, night vision

15

FIRESTORM VS FIREFLY

THE SETUP! Ronnie Raymond and Jason Rusch are on a field trip to Hub City's science lab when they see flames in the distance. The two young heroes sneak off and unite as Firestorm. They arrive at the mayor's burning mansion only to discover pyromaniac villain Firefly attempting to torch the building.

FIRESTORM

Ronnie Raymond and Jason Rusch couldn't be more different, but an atomic lab accident bonded them together, giving them the powers of the Firestorm matrix. Ronnie and Jason are now two heroes in one body with the power to manipulate the chemical makeup of inorganic matter.

SECRET FILE

Real Name	Ronald "Ronnie" Raymond & Jason Rusch
Weapons	Atomic powers
Occupation	Students
Height	6'1" (Raymond), 5'10" (Rusch)
Weight	179 lbs (Raymond), 165 lbs (Rusch)
Special Powers	Molecular control over inorganic matter, flight, fiery bolts of atomic energy

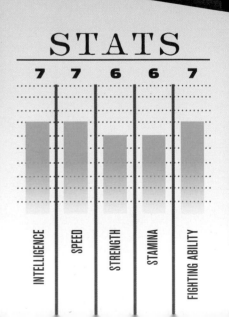

STATS

INTELLIGENCE	SPEED	STRENGTH	STAMINA	FIGHTING ABILITY
7	7	6	6	7

SHOWDOWN

As Firefly spreads the flames, Firestorm uses his matter-altering abilities to make the building's façade flame retardant. This makes the hotheaded Firefly fume with anger and turn his rage on Firestorm.

FIREFLY

Once a movie pyrotechnic stunt expert, Firefly became obsessed with fire. With his jet pack and flamethrower, Firefly wants to watch the world burn.

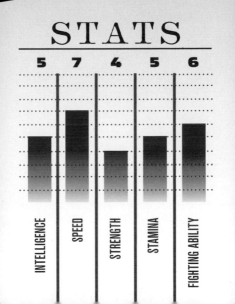

STATS

5	7	4	5	6
INTELLIGENCE	SPEED	STRENGTH	STAMINA	FIGHTING ABILITY

SECRET FILE

Real Name	Garfield Lynns
Weapons	Flamethrower
Occupation	Arsonist, villain
Height	5'11"
Weight	167 lbs
Special Powers	Jet pack-assisted flight, obsession with fire

ZATANNA VS SCARECROW

THE SETUP! The sinister Scarecrow floods the streets of Blüdhaven, a city nearby to Gotham City, with his noxious fear gas, driving its citizens into a hallucinating panic. Magical maven Zatanna happens to be in town performing in a stage show and catches a whiff of the Scarecrow's misdeeds.

ZATANNA

Following in her father's footsteps as a performer and crime fighter, Zatanna performs magic tricks on stage but also casts immensely powerful spells when needed by speaking backward.

SECRET FILE

Real Name	Zatanna Zatara
Weapons	Sorcery
Occupation	Magician
Height	5'7"
Weight	135 lbs
Special Powers	Magic and illusions

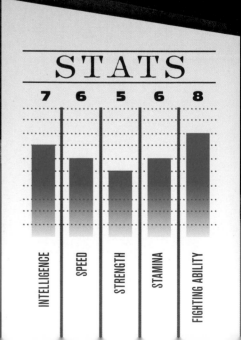

STATS

7	6	5	6	8
INTELLIGENCE	SPEED	STRENGTH	STAMINA	FIGHTING ABILITY

SHOWDOWN

Zatanna follows the trail of terrified people from her dressing room to the police station, where she finds Scarecrow. Before Zatanna can cast her spells and subdue the scoundrel, Scarecrow hits her with a concentrated dose of fear gas—causing Zatanna to believe her mouth has been sealed shut!

SCARECROW

As a respected professor at Gotham University, Dr. Jonathan Crane studied human reactions to fear. But his studies turned into an obsession and Scarecrow, his secret identity, was created.

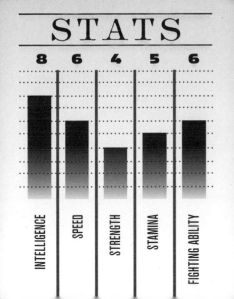

STATS

8	6	4	5	6
INTELLIGENCE	SPEED	STRENGTH	STAMINA	FIGHTING ABILITY

Real Name	Dr. Jonathan Crane
Weapons	Fear gas
Occupation	Former chemist, villain
Height	6'0"
Weight	120 lbs
Special Powers	Trained in chemistry, able to concoct hallucinogenic fear toxins

RED ARROW VS POISON IVY

THE SETUP! Red Arrow has taken the day to demonstrate safe archery skills at the Star City Hospital when a sickly sweet smell wafts past him. The hospital's plans to expand into a nearby wooded area have left a thorn in Ivy's side. She summons an enormous carnivorous plant to put an end to the expansion.

RED ARROW

Former sidekick Roy Harper learned all he could under his mentor, Green Arrow, before gaining his own spot in the Justice League. With unparalleled aim and a strong moral compass, Red Arrow is a respected member of the team.

SECRET FILE

Real Name	Roy Harper
Weapons	Bow and arrow
Occupation	Archer
Height	5'11"
Weight	195 lbs
Special Powers	Superb accuracy, an array of trick arrows

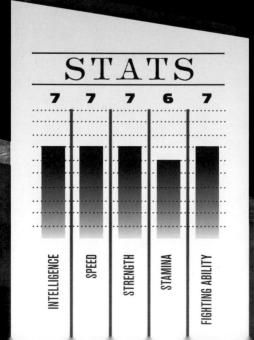

STATS

INTELLIGENCE	SPEED	STRENGTH	STAMINA	FIGHTING ABILITY
7	7	7	6	7

SHOWDOWN

As Red Arrow rushes the kids to safety, Poison Ivy wraps her plant's massive tendrils around the construction crew. Red Arrow lets loose a weedkiller arrow, which disintegrates the vicious vines. Ivy turns her terror on the archer. She commands the roots beneath his feet to rise around him, just as Red Arrow prepares to let a handcuff arrow fly.

POISON IVY

Poison Ivy sees herself as a hero to the Earth's plant life no matter how many human lives get in her way. With mastery over plants and their various toxins, Ivy is an alluringly dangerous foe.

STATS

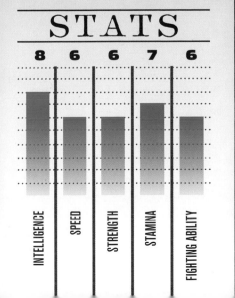

8	6	6	7	6
INTELLIGENCE	SPEED	STRENGTH	STAMINA	FIGHTING ABILITY

Real Name	Dr. Pamela Lillian Isley
Weapons	Toxins, poison kiss
Occupation	Botanist
Height	5'7"
Weight	133 lbs
Special Powers	Masterful acrobatics, fighting prowess, ability to control plant life

21

THE FLASH VS BANE

THE SETUP! Freshly escaped from Arkham Asylum and amped up on Venom, Bane savagely rampages through Central City. Bane has decided the home of The Flash is the perfect location for his next base of operations because he thinks The Flash will be an easy opponent to take down.

THE FLASH

A freak lab accident involving spilled chemicals and a perfectly timed lightning bolt connected police scientist Barry Allen to the Speed Force, an extra-dimensional energy that allows Barry to run faster than light.

SECRET FILE

Real Name	Bartholomew "Barry" Allen
Weapons	The Speed Force
Occupation	Police scientist
Height	5'11"
Weight	179 lbs
Special Powers	Super-speed, the ability to vibrate through solid objects

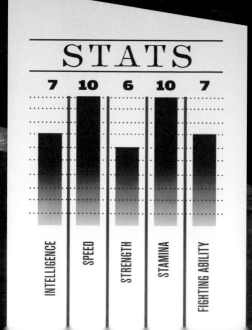

STATS

INTELLIGENCE	SPEED	STRENGTH	STAMINA	FIGHTING ABILITY
7	10	6	10	7

SHOWDOWN

To draw The Flash out, Bane storms The Flash Museum, trapping dozens of hostages inside. Bane challenges The Flash to find fifteen bombs hidden across the city in fifteen seconds or watch everything he loves go up in smoke and flame! Can The Flash uncover the locations of the villain's bombs before the city is demolished?

BANE

As a child, Bane was exposed to great pain and anger, which shaped him into an immensely strong and ruthless adult. Once free of his burdens, and with the assistance of tho chemical Venom, Bane seeks to conquer the greatest foes he can find.

STATS

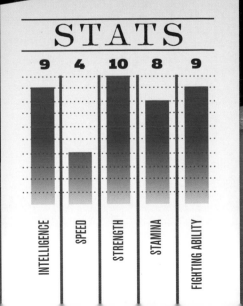

9	4	10	8	9
INTELLIGENCE	SPEED	STRENGTH	STAMINA	FIGHTING ABILITY

Real Name	Unknown
Weapons	Immense strength
Occupation	Criminal genius
Height	6'8"
Weight	350 lbs
Special Powers	Super-strength, durability while using Venom

23

ROBIN VS HUSH

THE SETUP! Thinking himself above the insane denizens of Arkham Asylum, Hush storms Blackgate Prison to release the general population and recruit himself an army. Hearing rumors of something going down at Blackgate, Batman tasks his protégé Robin to keep watch in one of the guard towers.

ROBIN

Tim Drake wasn't the first Robin, but he was the only one to deduce Batman's secret identity on his own. Seeing the potential in the amateur detective, the Dark Knight took Drake under his wing as his sidekick, the Boy Wonder!

SECRET FILE

Real Name	Tim Drake
Weapons	Batarang, bo staff
Occupation	Detective
Height	5'6"
Weight	145 lbs
Special Powers	Expert martial arts and computer knowledge

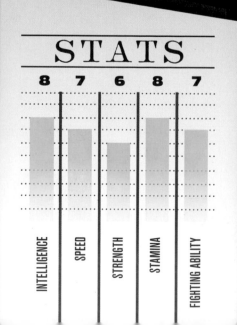

STATS

8	7	6	8	7
INTELLIGENCE	SPEED	STRENGTH	STAMINA	FIGHTING ABILITY

SHOWDOWN

After hours of keeping watch, a restless Robin picks up movement in the sewers with his infrared lenses. The Boy Wonder follows the lead and catches Hush in the prison's control room. Using one of his high-tech gadgets, Robin sets off an electromagnetic pulse that triggers the prison's lockdown—leaving Hush and the Boy Wonder locked in battle!

HUSH

Tommy Elliot had every chance of being a great man, but his misplaced childhood anger at Bruce Wayne became an obsession that drove him to manipulate Gotham City's worst criminals in a never-ending crusade against Batman.

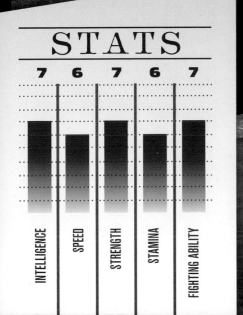

STATS

7	6	7	6	7
INTELLIGENCE	SPEED	STRENGTH	STAMINA	FIGHTING ABILITY

SECRET FILE

Real Name	Dr. Thomas "Tommy" Elliot
Weapons	Firearms, scalpel, switchblade
Occupation	Former surgeon
Height	6'1"
Weight	200 lbs
Special Powers	Great wealth, world-class training

SUPER-VILLAINS
SUPREME

Like a mirrored version of Superman, **BIZARRO** has an icy stare instead of heat vision, and spits flames rather than having freezing breath.

THE JOKER's arsenal of weapons reflects his odd sense of humor: acid-squirting lapel flowers and electrified joy buzzers.

LEX LUTHOR despises Superman, but is no match for him physically. To make up for this, Luthor often dons an advanced battle-suit powered by Kryptonite.

THE JOKER

BIZARRO

LEX LUTHOR

CATWOMAN

WHILE THE HEROES of the Justice League stand for what's right, these vile villains will do everything in their power to spread chaos and destruction. Often forced to form shaky alliances to combat the forces of good, these titans of trouble will stop at nothing to bring the world crashing down around them—and they'll do it with a smile, too!

Although **BANE** is feared for his Venom-assisted strength, his sharp tactical mind is what makes him a genuine threat.

CHEETAH once tried to steal Wonder Woman's Golden Lasso to add to her prized collection of pilfered artifacts.

Crime runs in **CAPTAIN COLD**'s family: his sister, Lisa Snart, clashed with The Flash as the Golden Glider.

ATROCITUS

CHEETAH

BANE

CAPTAIN COLD

HAWKGIRL VS CHEETAH

THE SETUP! In order to dig up dirt on Metropolis's social elite, Cheetah breaks into the Daily Planet building and steals the files containing information deemed too dangerous to print. While soaring high above the city on a late-night patrol, Hawkgirl spots the feline felon slinking out of the building's rooftop exit . . .

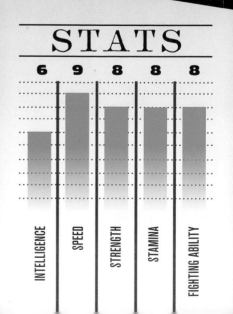

HAWKGIRL

The fierce warrior known as Hawkgirl has been reborn many times. In her current incarnation as a member of the Justice League, she uses her mighty wings and powerful mace to stand against injustice.

SECRET FILE

Real Name	Shayera Hall
Weapons	Mace, Nth metal belt
Occupation	Unknown
Height	5'7"
Weight	123 lbs
Special Powers	Flight, strength

STATS

INTELLIGENCE	SPEED	STRENGTH	STAMINA	FIGHTING ABILITY
6	9	8	8	8

SHOWDOWN

Hawkgirl glides down to catch Cheetah with a surprise strike, but the ruffle of her feathers is picked up by Cheetah's enhanced senses! With lightning speed, Cheetah leaps onto Hawkgirl's back. Not one to go down without a fight, Hawkgirl pulls out her mighty mace and a dizzying duel begins!

CHEETAH

Barbara Minerva used her extensive knowledge of archaeology to steal priceless artifacts for profit. When she stumbled on a lost temple in Africa, a ritual turned her into the ferocious Cheetah, as strong and fast as her animal namesake!

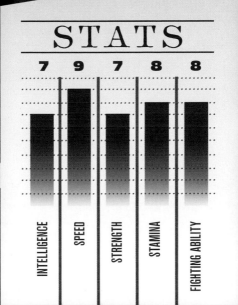

STATS

7	9	7	8	8
INTELLIGENCE	SPEED	STRENGTH	STAMINA	FIGHTING ABILITY

SECRET FILE

Real Name	Barbara Minerva
Weapons	Razor-sharp claws, prehensile tail
Occupation	Archaeologist
Height	5'9"
Weight	140 lbs
Special Powers	Heightened speed, strength, and senses

BLACK LIGHTNING **VS** KILLER CROC

THE SETUP!

Black Lightning is visiting Opal City for an academic conference when he picks up a police bulletin about an unusually large life-form in the sewers under the First National Bank. Descending underground, Black Lightning discovers Killer Croc, who is looking for trouble in a new town and is about to get it!

BLACK LIGHTNING

Black Lightning has committed his life to helping others. His Olympic training and ability generate intense bolts of electricity, which he uses to give bad guys quite the shock.

SECRET FILE

Real Name	Jefferson Pierce
Weapons	Lightning bolts
Occupation	Teacher
Height	6'1"
Weight	182 lbs
Special Powers	Ability to generate electricity, Olympic-level strength

STATS

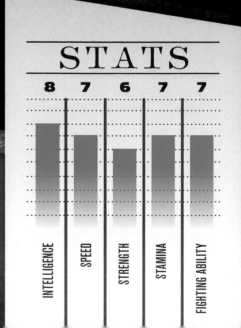

INTELLIGENCE	SPEED	STRENGTH	STAMINA	FIGHTING ABILITY
8	7	6	7	7

SHOWDOWN

The terrifyingly strong Killer Croc lashes out at the nimble former Olympian. Black Lightning zaps the criminal with bolts of electricity, but Croc's thick hide absorbs the blast. Knowing he's no match for Croc's strength, Black Lightning scans the sewer for an idea that will help him bring down Killer Croc!

KILLER CROC

Waylon Jones was born with thick, scaly skin and has since mutated to look even more like his namesake. Angry from years of bullying, Killer Croc stalks the sewers and swamps of Gotham City, ready for a fight.

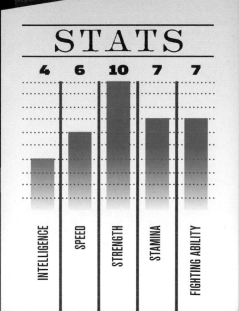

STATS

4	6	10	7	7
INTELLIGENCE	SPEED	STRENGTH	STAMINA	FIGHTING ABILITY

SECRET FILE

Real Name	Waylon Jones
Weapons	Razor-sharp teeth and claws
Occupation	Monstrous loner
Height	7'5"
Weight	686 lbs
Special Powers	Immense strength, impenetrable skin

31

BATWOMAN VS RĀ'S AL GHŪL

THE SETUP!
Batman enlists the help of the entire Batman family after receiving conflicting reports of where his archenemy Rā's al Ghūl plans to unleash his latest diabolical scheme. Batwoman is the first to spot Rā's al Ghūl. He and his minions are unloading barrels of poison into the reservoir of Gotham City!

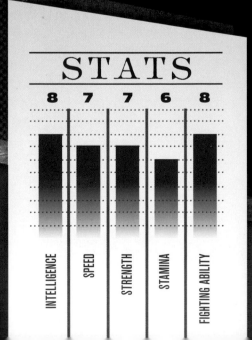

BATWOMAN

Socialite Kate Kane was once on track to join the U.S. Army before being discharged. Now, with Batman's blessing and the aid of her former-Marine father, Kate instills fear in the hearts of Gotham City's criminals.

SECRET FILE

Real Name	Katherine "Kate" Kane
Weapons	Batarangs, grappling hook
Occupation	Socialite
Height	5'11"
Weight	145 lbs
Special Powers	Proficient acrobat and hand-to-hand combatant

STATS

INTELLIGENCE	SPEED	STRENGTH	STAMINA	FIGHTING ABILITY
8	7	7	6	8

SHOWDOWN

From the shadows, Batwoman tosses a smoke grenade into the middle of the criminal activity. *POOF!* The crime fighter takes down the men in record time, but when the smoke clears, Rā's al Ghūl emerges untouched. The ancient adversary draws his scimitar and closes in to attack as Batwoman edges closer to the reservoir's edge.

RĀ'S AL GHŪL

Known as the Demon's Head, Rā's al Ghūl is a ruthless criminal mastermind whose sole mission is to cleanse the Earth and restart humanity in his own image. His criminal career spans thousands of years thanks to the life-restoring chemicals of the mysterious Lazarus Pits.

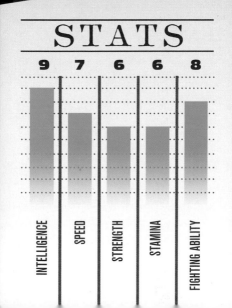

STATS

9	7	6	6	8
INTELLIGENCE	SPEED	STRENGTH	STAMINA	FIGHTING ABILITY

SECRET FILE

Real Name	Unknown
Weapons	Scimitar
Occupation	Criminal mastermind
Height	6'3"
Weight	160 lbs
Special Powers	Immortality granted by Lazarus Pits

SUPERMAN VS ARES

THE SETUP! Bored with manipulating human conflicts, Ares storms Superman's Arctic Fortress of Solitude in an attempt to seize the Man of Steel's inventory of weapons. Thousands of miles away, Superman hears the alarm and flies back to repel the mystical menace.

SUPERMAN

Rocketed to Earth from the doomed planet Krypton, baby Kal-El was given the name Clark by Ma and Pa Kent and was raised with strong morals. Armed with his sense of right and extraordinary abilities, Superman fights for truth and justice!

SECRET FILE

Real Name	Kal-El/Clark Kent
Weapons	None
Occupation	Reporter
Height	6'3"
Weight	235 lbs
Special Powers	Super-strength, super-speed, invulnerability, flight, heat vision

STATS

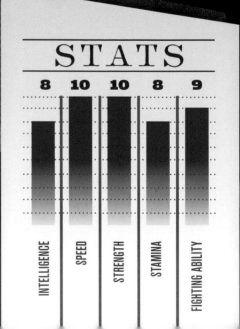

INTELLIGENCE	SPEED	STRENGTH	STAMINA	FIGHTING ABILITY
8	10	10	8	9

SHOWDOWN

Superman dive-bombs his fortress and smashes into Ares—*BOOM*—crashing them both through sheets of ice and crystal. Crawling from the rubble, Ares unsheathes his enchanted war axe and slashes at the Man of Steel, whose only weakness besides Kryptonite is magic!

ARES

The God of War from ancient Greek mythology, Ares has immense powers fueled by violence and hatred. When not clashing with his archenemy Wonder Woman, Ares manipulates conflict between humans and feeds off the chaos that ensues!

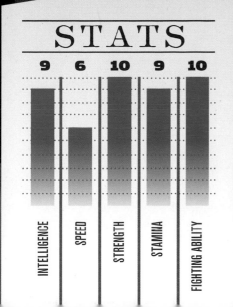

STATS

9	6	10	9	10
INTELLIGENCE	SPEED	STRENGTH	STAMINA	FIGHTING ABILITY

Real Name	Ares
Weapons	Axe, sword
Occupation	God of War
Height	6'10"
Weight	460 lbs
Special Powers	Mythical might and invulnerability

BLACK CANARY VS HARLEY QUINN

THE SETUP! Harley Quinn's fun always falters when the Joker is captured. Armed with a novelty-sized mallet, Harley sneaks into Arkham Asylum with a sinister scheme to spring out her precious "Mister J." This great escape plan is interrupted, however, when she finds Black Canary waiting for her.

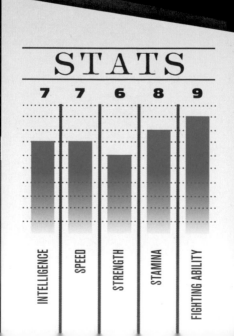

BLACK CANARY

An expert martial artist with an ear-piercing super-powered scream, Black Canary has trained with Batman and often fights crime in Gotham City alongside other female heroes like Batgirl and Huntress.

SECRET FILE

Real Name	Dinah Laurel Lance
Weapons	None
Occupation	Unknown
Height	5'5"
Weight	124 lbs
Special Powers	Sonic scream, martial arts mastery

STATS

7	7	6	8	9
INTELLIGENCE	SPEED	STRENGTH	STAMINA	FIGHTING ABILITY

SHOWDOWN

Harley giggles coyly and backs out of the room, but Black Canary isn't amused. The Justice Leaguer unleashes an earsplitting sonic cry that knocks Harley flat and rattles the walls around them. The crazed clown pulls out a pie and smashes it in Black Canary's face, silencing her cry!

HARLEY QUINN

Dr. Harleen Quinzel helped rehabilitate Gotham City's worst criminals as a psychologist at Arkham Asylum, until she met the Joker and fell in love. Now she devotes her life to helping her "Mister J" carry out his perilous pranks.

STATS

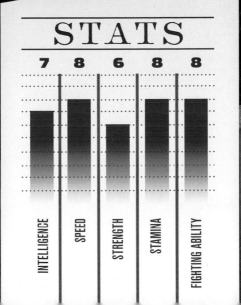

INTELLIGENCE	SPEED	STRENGTH	STAMINA	FIGHTING ABILITY
7	8	6	8	8

SECRET FILE

Real Name	Dr. Harleen Quinzel
Weapons	Pop-gun, giant mallet
Occupation	Joker's henchwoman
Height	5'7"
Weight	140 lbs
Special Powers	Gifted acrobat

37

RED TORNADO VS DEADSHOT

THE SETUP! During Red Tornado's routine sweep of downtown Happy Harbor, his sensors pick up a large stash of weapons in a derelict building. Before the android hero can attempt to destroy the dangerous cargo, he enters Deadshot's crosshairs.

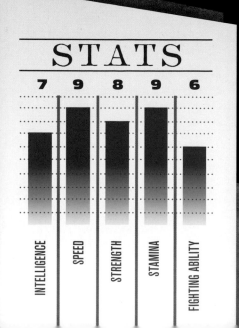

RED TORNADO

Created by a mad scientist to destroy the Justice League, Red Tornado overcame his programming and became a trusted member of the team.

SECRET FILE

Real Name	John Smith
Weapons	Powerful android body
Occupation	Android hero
Height	6'1"
Weight	325 lbs
Special Powers	Ability to produce gale-force winds and cyclones

STATS

INTELLIGENCE	SPEED	STRENGTH	STAMINA	FIGHTING ABILITY
7	9	8	9	6

SHOWDOWN

Deadshot expertly fires off a few shots, but Red Tornado deflects the bullets with a miniature tornado. Focused on his objective, the advanced android generates a massive gust of wind, scattering Deadshot and his stockpile of weapons. The sharp-eyed sniper scrambles to his feet and takes aim at his bright-red bull's-eye!

DEADSHOT

Deadshot is the best marksman in the world and lacks nearly any sense of a moral compass. If the price is right, Deadshot will take the job—and the shot.

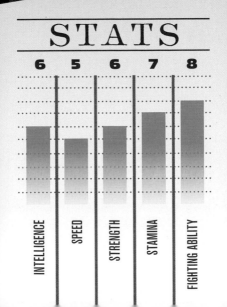

STATS

6	5	6	7	8
INTELLIGENCE	SPEED	STRENGTH	STAMINA	FIGHTING ABILITY

SECRET FILE

Real Name	Floyd Lawton
Weapons	Wrist-mounted pistols
Occupation	Mercenary
Height	6'1"
Weight	193 lbs
Special Powers	Perfect aim

HUNTRESS VS TWO-FACE

THE SETUP! Huntress, the Batman family's resident loner, catches Two-Face flipping his coin to decide whether or not to rob the Gotham City Museum's new exhibit. She knocks Two-Face's coin out of the air with a well-aimed arrow from her crossbow, and then moves in to knock out the unhinged former DA.

HUNTRESS

Raised among organized crime, Helena Bertinelli rejected her path and dedicated her life to justice— although her methods of handling criminals sometimes put her at odds with Batman.

SECRET FILE

Real Name	Helena Bertinelli
Weapons	Miniature crossbow
Occupation	Vigilante
Height	5'11"
Weight	148 lbs
Special Powers	Expert gymnast and fighter

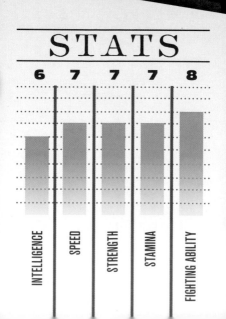

STATS

	6	7	7	7	8
	INTELLIGENCE	SPEED	STRENGTH	STAMINA	FIGHTING ABILITY

SHOWDOWN

Panicked over the loss of his "lucky" coin, Two-Face orders his goons to attack. His hired muscle is no match for Huntress, who quickly dispatches them. Huntress then turns her attention to Two-Face, and the two engage in a tense battle.

TWO-FACE

District attorney Harvey Dent was an honest man until a mob boss threw acid on his face, scarring him and unlocking a chaotic double personality. Now the duality-obsessed crime boss relics on his two-headed coin to make decisions for good or evil.

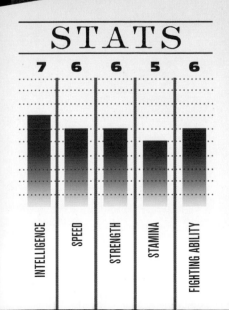

STATS

7	6	6	5	6
INTELLIGENCE	SPEED	STRENGTH	STAMINA	FIGHTING ABILITY

Real Name	Harvey Dent
Weapons	Twin firearms
Occupation	Former district attorney
Height	6'0"
Weight	182 lbs
Special Powers	Dangerous split personality

MARTIAN MANHUNTER VS BIZARRO

THE SETUP! The backward brute Bizarro is accidentally beamed into the Justice League satellite when the teleporter mistakes him for Superman! Martian Manhunter, permanent resident on the satellite and the League's mission coordinator, immediately confronts the bumbling intruder.

MARTIAN MANHUNTER

Martian Manhunter was one of the last surviving Martians after a plague wiped out most of his planet's intelligent life. Mistakenly teleported to Earth, Manhunter joined the Justice League to make sure the humans of Earth never suffered the same fate as his people.

SECRET FILE

Real Name	J'onn J'onzz / John Jones
Weapons	None
Occupation	Unknown
Height	6'7"
Weight	300 lbs
Special Powers	Telepathy, shape-shifting, intangibility, super-strength

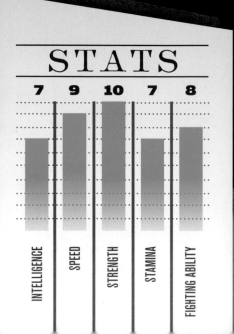

STATS

INTELLIGENCE	SPEED	STRENGTH	STAMINA	FIGHTING ABILITY
7	9	10	7	8

SHOWDOWN

Possessing equal strength and speed, Martian Manhunter is an even match for Bizarro. But the flawed doppelgänger's mixed-up mental state is indecipherable to Manhunter, who normally reads his opponents' minds during battle. That leaves Manhunter unsure of Bizarro's next move!

BIZARRO

The twisted terror Bizarro is a distorted mirror image of Superman with all of the power and none of the responsibility. Created by Lex Luthor to defeat the Man of Steel, Bizarro flies in and out of trouble following his flawed logic.

STATS

2	9	10	8	7
INTELLIGENCE	SPEED	STRENGTH	STAMINA	FIGHTING ABILITY

Real Name	None
Weapons	None
Occupation	Simple-minded brute
Height	6'3"
Weight	225 lbs
Special Powers	Freeze vision, flame breath, immense strength, indestructibility

VIXEN VS THE PENGUIN

THE SETUP! Vixen has tracked the Penguin, a fugitive from the law, to the Iceberg Lounge, where he is raiding his stash of cash to prepare to fly the coop! Adopting the slinky stealth of a fox, Vixen corners the Penguin and prepares to pounce.

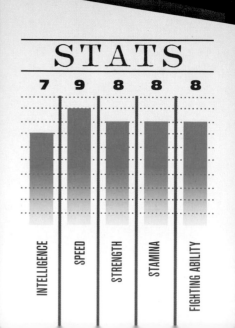

VIXEN

Supermodel Mari McCabe is the latest in her family to use the Tantu Totem, a magical artifact that lets the user access the skills of any animal—such as the strength of an elephant, the speed of a cheetah—to protect the innocent.

SECRET FILE

Real Name	Mari Jiwe McCabe
Weapons	Tantu Totem
Occupation	Supermodel
Height	5'7"
Weight	149 lbs
Special Powers	Ability to mimic the abilities of any animal she chooses

STATS

INTELLIGENCE	SPEED	STRENGTH	STAMINA	FIGHTING ABILITY
7	9	8	8	8

44

SHOWDOWN

With his fine feathers ruffled, the Penguin pulls out one of his trick umbrellas. As Vixen leaps around the room with amazing agility, the Penguin frantically fires tranquilizer darts, hoping to hit his target!

THE PENGUIN

Frequently bullied as a child, the Penguin grew to embrace his birdlike features and direct his anger into controlling the criminal underworld. Even with his array of assault umbrellas and dangerous henchmen, this criminal bird still manages to mingle with high society.

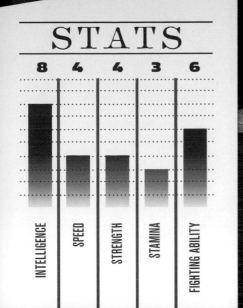

STATS

INTELLIGENCE	SPEED	STRENGTH	STAMINA	FIGHTING ABILITY
8	4	4	3	6

SECRET FILE

Real Name	Oswald Chesterfield Cobblepot
Weapons	Trick umbrellas
Occupation	Iceberg Lounge owner
Height	5'2"
Weight	175 lbs
Special Powers	Master manipulator

BATMAN VS LEX LUTHOR

THE SETUP!

With Superman on an off-world mission, Batman travels to Metropolis following a tip that malicious mastermind Lex Luthor is orchestrating an attack on the city. Using his high-tech gadgets, the Dark Knight penetrates the LexCorp Tower and finds the evil genius in his underground laboratory.

BATMAN

A vigilante molded from childhood trauma, Batman vows to protect the citizens of Gotham City. His considerable intelligence, wealth, and skills aid him in his crime-fighting crusade, creating a range of gadgets that deftly dispense justice.

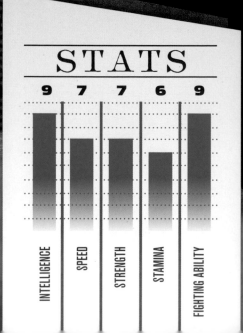

STATS

9	7	7	6	9
INTELLIGENCE	SPEED	STRENGTH	STAMINA	FIGHTING ABILITY

SECRET FILE

Real Name	Bruce Wayne
Weapons	Batarangs, grappling hook, smoke pellets
Occupation	Entrepreneur
Height	6'2"
Weight	210 lbs
Special Powers	World-class detective, skilled martial artist

SHOWDOWN

Lex Luthor has created a robot that looks like Superman with the intention of blaming the real Man of Steel for the havoc it will wreak. Luthor orders it to destroy the Dark Knight, but Batman delivers an explosive Batarang, blowing it and Luthor's rage sky-high! Donning his armored battle-suit, Lex Luthor charges at the Caped Crusader.

LEX LUTHOR

While Lex Luthor's immense intellect and unlimited resources could make the world a better place, they're more often put to use serving his selfish ego. Luthor's unending quest for dominance results in schemes to make Superman look like a zero—and make himself look like a hero!

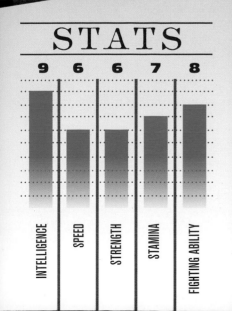

STATS

INTELLIGENCE	SPEED	STRENGTH	STAMINA	FIGHTING ABILITY
9	6	6	7	8

Real Name	Lex Luthor
Weapons	Battle-suit
Occupation	Scientist, businessman
Height	5'10"
Weight	200 lbs
Special Powers	Incredible wealth

EXPERT PICKS

GREEN LANTERN (JOHN STEWART) VS. THE JOKER

THE WINNER: GREEN LANTERN (JOHN STEWART)
The Joker is used to clashing with Batman, an extremely intelligent hero—without super-powers. Once Green Lantern finds the Joker, he envelops him in an airtight energy-construct cage, holding the Joker long enough to lock him in an Arkham cell.

WONDER WOMAN VS. ATROCITUS

THE WINNER: WONDER WOMAN
Wonder Woman's Golden Lasso of Truth is a dangerous weapon against a being of pure rage. When it's slipped around Atrocitus's body, the alien is forced to face the true motivation for his hate, debilitating him until Wonder Woman can turn him over to the Green Lantern Corps.

NIGHTWING VS. CATWOMAN

THE WINNER: CATWOMAN
Nightwing may not understand Batman's relationship with Catwoman, but he still respects Batman's orders. With Catwoman's stolen goods recovered, Nightwing stands down, allowing Catwoman to escape yet again.

GREEN LANTERN (HAL JORDAN) VS. CAPTAIN COLD

THE WINNER: CAPTAIN COLD
Captain Cold calculated correctly. Green Lantern makes rescuing the civilians a priority, and it take his complete focus. Captain Cold uses the distraction to slip into a manhole and ices it shut behind him.

CYBORG VS. MAN-BAT

WINNER: CYBORG
Man-Bat is dangerously out of control. Seeing Man-Bat's poor reaction to the sound of the crowd, Cyborg hits him with a sonic blast, overloading his sensitive hearing and knocking him out cold.

FIRESTORM VS. FIREFLY

WINNER: FIRESTORM
Firefly has an itchy trigger finger when it comes to his flamethrower, but his weapon is useless without fuel. Firestorm uses his matter-altering powers to transmute the remaining fuel into flame-retardant gel, causing Firefly to douse his own blaze.

ZATANNA VS. SCARECROW

THE WINNER: ZATANNA
When Scarecrow's fear gas causes Zatanna to hallucinate that her mouth is fusing shut, she briefly panics. But the sound of her own frightened gasp reminds her it is just an illusion. She quickly uses her magic to "kcol eht Worceracs yawa rof doog."

RED ARROW VS. POISON IVY

THE WINNER: POISON IVY
Red Arrow may be a perfect shot, but you can't shoot pheromone toxins. Poison Ivy releases plant chemicals that put everyone to sleep, including the heroic archer. It gives her enough time to trash the construction equipment and plant a kiss on Red Arrow's cheek before escaping.

THE FLASH VS. BANE

THE WINNER: THE FLASH
The Flash's intimate knowledge of his hometown makes finding fifteen bombs in fifteen seconds a breeze! Before the countdown is over, The Flash vibrates through the museum wall, disconnects Bane's Venom supply, and ends the villain's siege with a flurry of punches.

ROBIN VS. HUSH

THE WINNER: ROBIN
When Hush fights Batman, he preys on their shared childhood, but Robin has no such sentimentality. He ends the fight quickly by dropping a blinding smoke pellet, and with his infrared goggles, takes an easy swing with his bo staff to knock Hush out.

HAWKGIRL VS. CHEETAH

THE WINNER: CHEETAH
As Hawkgirl and Cheetah plummet toward the pavement, Hawkgirl lashes out with her mace, destroying the data that Cheetah has stolen. With her plot foiled, Cheetah leaps off Hawkgirl's back just before they crash into a building and escapes while Hawkgirl recovers from the impact.

BLACK LIGHTNING VS. KILLER CROC

THE WINNER: BLACK LIGHTNING
Black Lightning's electrical powers may not affect Croc's thick skin on their own, but Croc is standing in three feet of sewer water surrounded by metal pipes. Black Lightning grabs hold of a nearby ladder and lets loose a few thousand volts, paralyzing Croc.

BATWOMAN VS. RĀ'S AL GHŪL

THE WINNER: RĀ'S AL GHŪL
Without a sword of her own, Batwoman blocks Rā's al Ghūl's thrusts with her reinforced gauntlets. She's at a clear disadvantage until a well-timed shot with her grappling hook dislodges Rā's al Ghūl's sword. Without a weapon, Rā's al Ghūl leaps into the reservoir, taking a fall only he can survive.

SUPERMAN VS. ARES

THE WINNER: SUPERMAN
Superman may have a weakness against magic, but the Man of Steel can't allow his weapons to fall into evil hands. Summoning all of his strength, Superman knocks Ares into the path of the Phantom Zone Projector, trapping the God of War in an alternate dimension where he can do no harm.

BLACK CANARY VS. HARLEY QUINN

THE WINNER: HARLEY QUINN
In a fair fight, Black Canary's martial arts skills would trump Harley's acrobatics. Unfortunately, Harley never fights fair. While Black Canary cleans pie out of her eyes, Harley smashes the Joker's cell—weakened by Black Canary's sonic scream—and absconds with her "Mister J."

RED TORNADO VS. DEADSHOT

THE WINNER: DEADSHOT
Having an indestructible android body and backups of your personality sometimes makes Red Tornado too bold. Deadshot loads explosive ammo, which detonates on impact with Red Tornado's whirlwinds and incapacitates the robot long enough for Deadshot to grab his weapons and run.

HUNTRESS VS. TWO-FACE

THE WINNER: HUNTRESS
Their bullets and crossbow bolts ricochet off priceless artifacts and make them worthless! The Huntress lures the gangster into the dinosaur room, where one perfectly aimed crossbow bolt sends a T. rex skeleton crashing down on top of Two-Face, pinning him until the cops arrive to dig him out.

MARTIAN MANHUNTER VS. BIZARRO

THE WINNER: BIZARRO
Martian Manhunter may have super-human strength, but he has a much more common weakness: fire. Bizarro coughs up a ball of flame breath at Manhunter, defeating the Justice Leaguer before once again taking the teleporter to parts unknown.

VIXEN VS. THE PENGUIN

THE WINNER: VIXEN
The Penguin puts up a good fight, peppering the room with darts and bullets from his various trick umbrellas. Vixen nimbly avoids the projectiles before taking on the power and mass of a penguin's worst nightmare: the orca whale. One belly flop puts the Penguin on ice.

BATMAN VS. LEX LUTHOR

THE WINNER: BATMAN
Luthor expects his powerful exosuit to give him the upper hand, but the Dark Knight deploys the high-voltage Bat-taser, which overloads the armor. Taking advantage of the disabled suit, Batman applies a fast-acting sealant foam to clog the joints of the exosuit, trapping Luthor in his own suit.

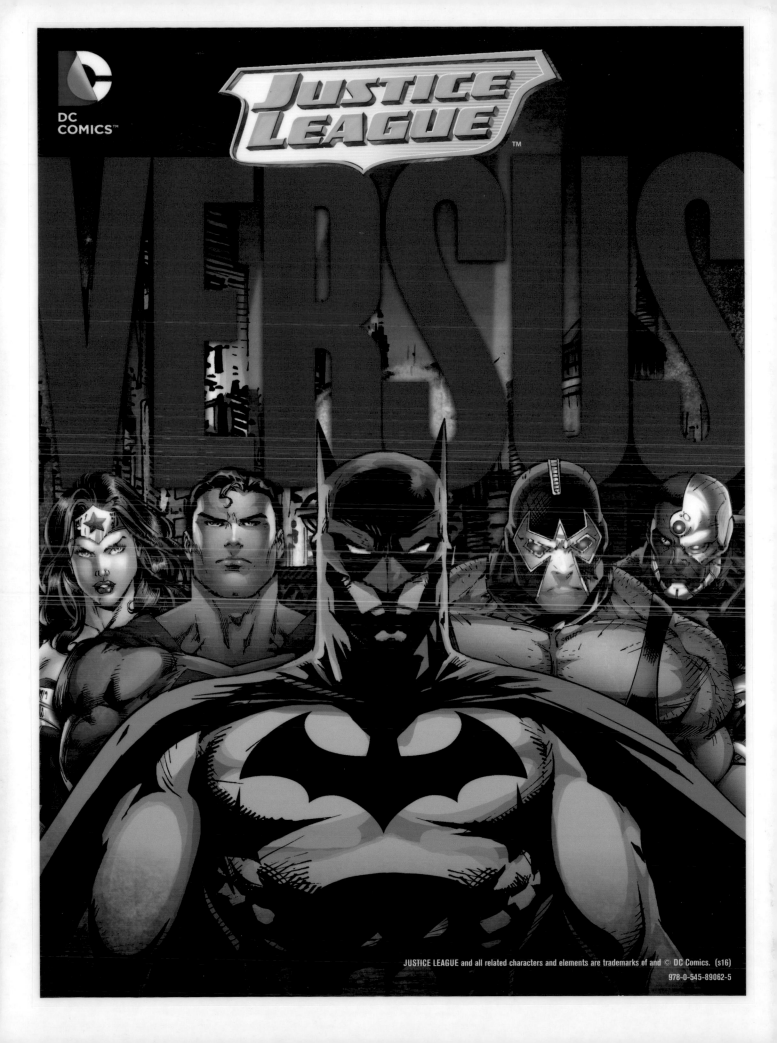

978-0-545-89062-5